Cat
Patrol

Paul May

Illustrated by Peter Bailey

Series reading consultant: Prue Goodwin,
Reading and Language Information Centre,
University of Reading

CAT PATROL
A CORGI PUPS BOOK

First publication in Great Britain

PRINTING HISTORY
Corgi Pups edition published 2001

ISBN 0 552 54938 X

Set in 18/25 Bembo Schoolbook

Corgi Pups Books are published by Transworld Publishers,
61–63 Uxbridge Road, Ealing, London W5 5SA,
a division of the Random House Group Ltd,
in Australia by Random House Australia (Pty) Ltd,
20 Alfred Street, Milsons Point, Sydney, NSW 2061, Australia
in New Zealand by Random House New Zealand Ltd,
18 Poland Road, Glenfield, Auckland 10, New Zealand
and in South Africa by Random House (Pty) Ltd,
Endulini, 5a Jubilee Road, Parktown 2193, South Africa

Printed and bound in Denmark by
Nørhaven Paperback, Viborg

Contents

www.booksattransworld.co.uk/childrens

Chapter One

Ben watched the robin fly down
from the apple tree. He held his
breath as the little bird hopped
across the grass. It looked
quickly from side to side, then it
flew onto Ben's hand and
pecked at the crumbs there.

"Ben!" called his big sister, Laura. "They're here. Come and see."

The robin vanished over the wall into the garden of the empty house next door.

Birds had built their nests in the
jungle that had grown there,
and Ben had been watching
them all through the long
summer holiday. But now the
new neighbours had arrived.

Ben walked slowly to the front door.

"Ben," called Mum. "Come and say hello to Mr and Mrs Jones."

"Very pleased to meet you," said Mr Jones. He smiled down at Ben from a brown, wrinkled face. Then he turned to Mum. "The garden's a bit of a mess, I'm afraid. But  we'll soon sort it out. I'll get cracking right away."

Ben wanted to tell Mr Jones that the birds loved the garden just the way it was. Mrs Jones didn't give him a chance.

"Now then, you two," she said to Laura and Ben. "You must meet Sammy." She lifted a large basket from the back seat of the car.

"Meet Samuel Pennyfeather Lexington Star the Third," she said, proudly, "Sammy for short."

Ben was horrified. Sammy was a cat — the most enormous cat he had ever seen. It stared at him through the wire of its basket. Its eyes were cold and blue. It yawned, and its teeth were like razors.

"He's a pedigree Siamese. Isn't he handsome?" said Mrs Jones.

"But . . . but . . . it's a *cat*!" Ben stammered. He turned and fled indoors.

"Don't worry, Ben," said Mum at teatime. "I'm sure Sammy is a very nice cat."

"There's no such thing as a nice cat," said Ben. "Cats kill birds. You know they do."

Chapter Two

Early the next morning Ben
looked down from his bedroom
window into the neighbours'
garden. The jungle had gone.
The grass had been shaved and
the bushes hacked down.

A door opened, and the cat
stalked out of the house. It leapt
onto the wall and looked down
into Ben's garden.

Ben rushed into Laura's room.
"Quick!" he said, shaking her.
"We'll have to start a cat
patrol."

"A what?" said Laura,
sleepily.

"A cat patrol," repeated Ben. "The birds aren't safe. They can't live next door any more, and now that cat's looking at *our* garden. It looks hungry."

"He's a *pet*, Ben," said Laura. "I bet he only eats best quality cat food. Don't worry about him."

Ben wouldn't go indoors for his breakfast. He sat on a chair by the back door to eat his toast. He watched a blackbird trying to tug a worm from the grass. Suddenly, the blackbird dropped the worm and flew up into the bushes. It sat on a branch, chattering in alarm.

Sparrows fluttered into the air.
There was a rustling in the
flowerbed, and the cat appeared.

"No!" cried Ben. The cat had
something in its mouth. Ben felt
his heart miss a beat. He
thought it was his robin.

"Drop it!" Ben shouted.
"Leave it alone!"

"It's all right," said Laura. "It's
only a mouse."

The cat turned and jumped
onto the wall. It lay there,
gazing down into the garden
with its strange blue eyes. The
mouse's tail was hanging from
the corner of its mouth. The cat
crunched and swallowed. The
tail vanished.

"It's *not* all right," said Ben.
"That cat's a killer. I told you it
was. It'll kill birds, too, if we
don't stop it. We've *got* to have a
cat patrol. We'll have to watch
all the time."

"Don't be silly," said Laura,
"we can't watch *all* the time."

"Yes we can. If you help. We'll
take turns."

Laura gave in. She sat reading
her book in the garden, while
the cat slept on the top of the
wall in the warm sun. Late in
the afternoon they heard Mrs
Jones calling, "Here, Sammy!
Teatime!"

"I'm going in," said Laura. "The birds are safe now."

Ben waited. He didn't trust the cat. He waited until he heard Mrs Jones say, "Good boy, Sammy," and then he stood up.

Right at that moment a bird swooped through the garden. Its wings almost brushed Ben's face.

The bird crashed into the bushes, hopped a little way onto the grass, and then sat very still.

Chapter Three

"Hello, little bird," said Ben
softly. "What's the matter?"

He knelt down and reached
out his hand. The bird took off
in a sudden flurry of wings. It
flapped across the garden.

Then it hit a bush, and fell to
the ground.

Ben looked for the cat. He couldn't see it anywhere.

"Don't be frightened, little bird," said Ben. "I won't hurt you."

The bird's eyes were wild and scared. Ben lay down. This time, the bird didn't move.

Ben reached out slowly and
closed his hand around soft
feathers.

A small, fierce face glared from
between his fingers. It wasn't a
sparrow, or a blackbird, or a
robin. Ben didn't know what it
was. He carried the bird
carefully into the house.

"Look, Mum," said Ben. "I've found a bird. He's warm. I can feel his heart beating."

"Let me see," said Mum. "Did the cat get him? I thought you were watching."

"But it wasn't the cat," said
Ben. "He crashed in the garden.
I saw everything. He tried to fly
away, but then he crashed again."

"Perhaps he's a baby," said
Laura. "Perhaps he's lost his
mum."

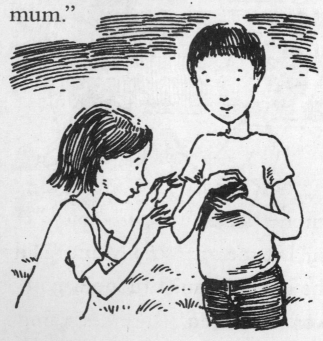

"I'm going to look after him,"
said Ben, "until he's big enough
to fly properly. I can, Mum,
can't I? There's an old hamster
cage in the shed. He'll be safe
there."

"I don't know," said Mum.
"Perhaps we should take him to
the vet."

"No!" said Ben. Early in the
summer he had found an
injured sparrow. They had taken
it to the vet, and the vet had
told them that the kindest thing

to do was to put the sparrow to
sleep. Ben knew what *that*
meant. The sparrow was dead.

"Please, Mum," said Ben.

"Well, all right then," said
Mum. "But he's a wild bird, Ben.
He can't be a pet. You know
that, don't you?"

Ben nodded.

"Right," said Mum. "Let's try and find out what kind of bird he is."

Ben looked at the pictures in the bird book, but he couldn't see his bird anywhere. The bird sat in the cage beside them. Ben had given him some water in a saucer, but he didn't drink.

"Let me see," said Laura.
"There! I bet that's him. I bet
he's a baby one of those."

The bird in the picture was a
kestrel.

"He's not *really* the same,"
Ben said.

"I don't know," said Mum.
"Your little bird does look fierce,
and that beak is *very* sharp."

"What do kestrels eat, then?"
asked Ben. Laura frowned. She
wasn't quite sure what some of
the words meant. Then she
found the place.

"'Mice,'" she read, "'and voles, and sometimes small birds.' But he couldn't! He's too little."

"What else?" said Ben. "There must be something."

"I've got it! 'Worms and large insects.' We'll collect some after tea."

They dug for a long time
before they found two skinny
worms. Ben poked them
between the bars of the cage.

The little bird didn't move. He
didn't even look at the worms.
He glared at them out of his
small black eyes.

Ben and Laura tried other things. They tried bread, and nuts, and berries from the hedge. None of them were any good.

"I'm going in," said Laura. "This is a waste of time."

"No, it's not," said Ben. "We've got to keep trying."

But Laura had already gone.

The evening sky was full of
birds, wheeling and swooping.
Then a dark shape appeared on
top of the wall. The cat.

"I can't let you go," Ben said
to the bird. "You need to be able
to fly properly first. You've got to
eat something. Why won't you
eat?"

Chapter Four

All the next day, Ben sat in the
garden with the little bird by his
side, keeping watch for the cat.

After lunch, Mum and Laura
went to visit Mr and Mrs Jones.

"They're very nice," Mum
said when she returned. "I told
them about your cat patrol. Mrs
Jones said you mustn't worry.
Sammy never catches birds."

"Huh!" said Ben.

"I was right about the cat food, too," said Laura. "He only eats *Smoked Salmon Supreme*. And he's not allowed out at night in case he catches cold."

Mum laughed. "At least the birds are safe at night. And how is this little fellow?"

"He's all right," said Ben.

"Has he eaten anything?"

"Not yet," said Ben, "but he will."

"One more day," said Mum. "Then we're taking him to the vet."

That night, Ben couldn't
sleep. He woke in the darkness
and saw the little bird staring at
the moonlit sky.

"You want to be free, don't
you?" whispered Ben.

"You nearly did it the day I found you. I bet if you had one more try you could find your mum all on your own. I won't let them take you to the vet. I won't."

When it began to grow light, Ben dressed quickly, and tiptoed downstairs. In the garden, all the birds were singing.

"It's safe," thought Ben. "The stupid cat's indoors."

"Ben!" called Laura, "What are you doing?" She was wearing wellington boots over her pyjama trousers.

"He can't stay in that cage," said Ben. "He hates it."

"Don't, Ben."

"You don't know anything. I found him."

"*Ben!*"

Ben opened his hands. For a second the bird sat still.

Then, suddenly, he was off. This time he skimmed over the top of the tallest plants in the flowerbed.

"Go on!" urged Ben. "Higher!"

The little bird hit the fence, and fluttered to the ground.

Laura screamed. "Ben! The cat!"

Ben looked up. The cat came over the wall in a pale blur.

Ben raced towards the little bird, but the cat got there first.

Ben flung himself on top of it.
The bird was in the cat's mouth.
"Drop him!" screamed Ben.
"Let him go!"

Mum came running from the
house. "Ben?" she said. "What's
going on?"

Ben stood up. His face was
bleeding where the cat had
scratched him. In his hand was
the bird. It was still warm, and
its heart was beating fast. Ben
felt tears come into his eyes.

"Why did you let him out?"
said Laura. "You were the one
who wanted the cat patrol. You
were the one who wanted to
keep him in the cage. You . . ."

"Laura!" said Mum, sharply.

"He was miserable," said Ben.
"I know he was. He hates it in
that cage. And I don't want him
to go to the vet."

Mum took the little bird in
her hands. "We'll have to take
him," she said. "There's nothing
else we can do. We'll go this
afternoon."

"No!" cried Ben. "You know
what the vet will do."

"Don't be silly, Ben. The vet
might be able to tell us how
to make him
better."

"Or he'll put
him to sleep,"
said Ben.

"I'm sorry," said Mum. "But
you can't just keep him in that
cage while he gets thinner and
thinner. You know you can't."

Chapter Five

It was late in the afternoon
when Mum came into the
garden. Ben felt sick. It was
time to go to the vet.

Then he saw that Mum had
someone with her. It was Mr
Jones.

"I'm really very sorry," he said
to Ben. "Your mum told me
what happened. Maybe I can
help. I know a little about birds.
Will you let me look?"

Ben looked up at Mr Jones's wrinkled face. His eyes were kind. Ben took the bird from the cage.

"I found him in the garden," he said. "But he won't eat anything. I think he's going to die."

Mr Jones took the little bird from Ben's hands. He looked into its fierce eyes. Then, very gently, he stretched out its wings. They were long and pointed. He stretched out its tail. It forked at the end.

"What a fine little bird," he said.

"But what kind of a bird?" said Ben.

"I thought he might be a
baby kestrel," said Laura.

"I see what you mean," said
Mr Jones. "That beak would be
perfect for catching mice if it
was bigger. But he's not a baby
at all. He's a swift – a grown-up
swift. Look. Up there in the sky."

Ben, Laura and Mum looked up. High in the afternoon sky, birds were wheeling and swooping.

"Swifts," said Mr Jones. "They're catching insects. They only eat when they're flying. That's why he wouldn't eat your worms."

"You mean my little bird is one of them?" said Ben. It didn't seem possible.

"He certainly is."

"Then why can't he fly?"

"I'm sure he can," said Mr Jones. "But you'll have to help him."

"Me?" said Ben. "But how?"

"Swifts are wonderful birds," said Mr Jones. "They never, ever land on the ground. If they land by accident, then they can get stuck. Like this little chap."

"He tried to take off again," said Ben, "but he couldn't get high enough."

 "And then Sammy nearly got him," said Laura.

Ben shivered as he remembered the terrible moment. Just then Mrs Jones came round the side of the house.

"I'm *so* sorry about Sammy," she said. "As soon as I heard, I went straight out and bought him this." She showed Ben a large bell on a pink ribbon.

Then she saw the bird peeping
out between Mr Jones's fingers.

"Oh, look!" she exclaimed. "It's
a swift! Isn't he beautiful!"

Mrs Jones turned to Ben. "We
used to live in Africa," she said.
"That's where swifts spend the
winter. Imagine this little bird
flying all the way to Africa!"

Ben looked at Mr and Mrs
Jones. Nobody who knew so
much about birds could be *all* bad.

And the thought of the terrible
Sammy wearing a bell on a pink
ribbon made him smile. Sammy's
hunting days were over. The cat
patrol had done its job.

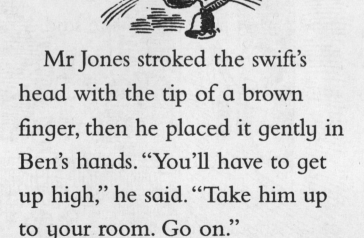

Mr Jones stroked the swift's
head with the tip of a brown
finger, then he placed it gently in
Ben's hands. "You'll have to get
up high," he said. "Take him up
to your room. Go on."

Ben climbed the stairs to his
bedroom, and looked down into
the garden.

"Count to three, and then
throw him," called Mr Jones.
"Throw him as high as you
can."

Ben looked at the swift. The
swift glared at him. They all
counted: Mum and Laura, Mr
and Mrs Jones, and Ben.

"One . . . two . . . three . . ."
Ben threw.

Above their heads, the swift
opened its wings.

It cut through the air, higher
and higher, until it was just one
of a thousand birds wheeling
and soaring.

Ben laughed with the joy of
it. He thought of his bird flying
on and on, all the way to Africa.
He looked from his empty hands
to the crowded sky.

"That was the best thing," he
said. "The best thing ever."

THE END